Plants vs. Zombies

GROWN SWEET HOME #1

ABDO
Spotlight

DARK HORSE COMICS

PopCap

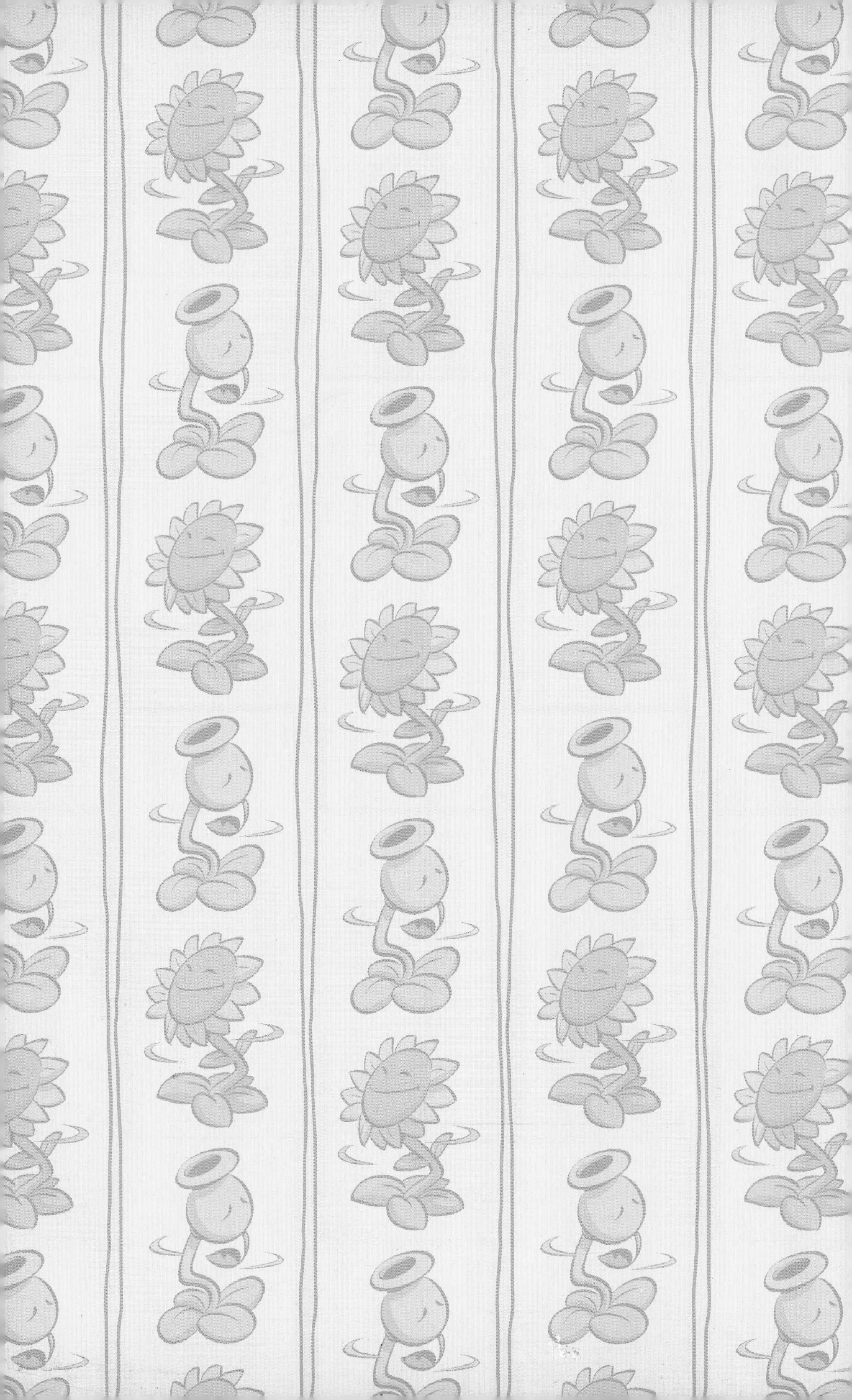

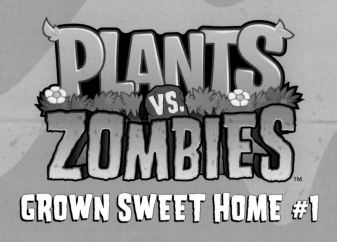

PLANTS VS. ZOMBIES™

GROWN SWEET HOME #1

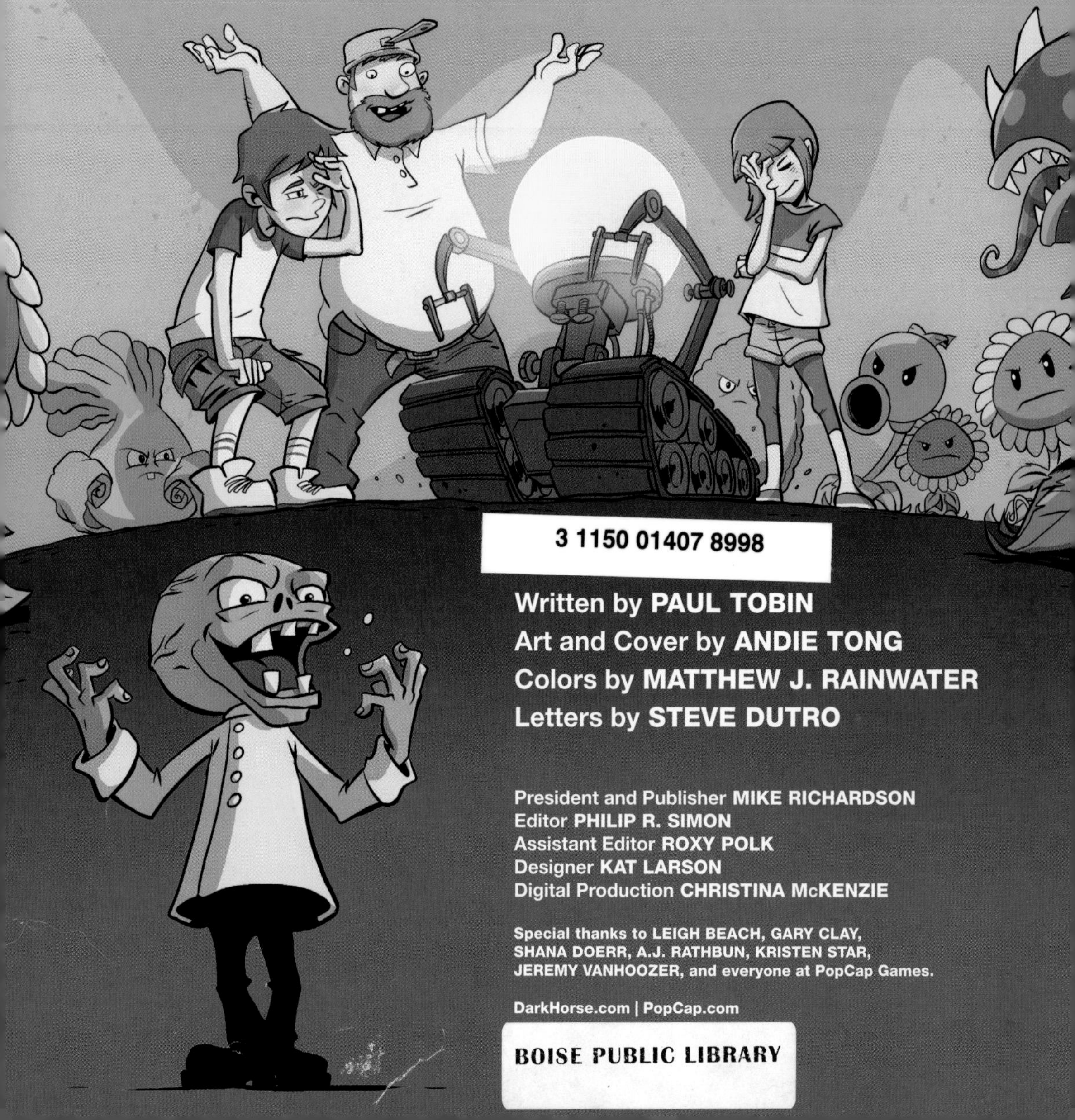

Written by **PAUL TOBIN**
Art and Cover by **ANDIE TONG**
Colors by **MATTHEW J. RAINWATER**
Letters by **STEVE DUTRO**

President and Publisher **MIKE RICHARDSON**
Editor **PHILIP R. SIMON**
Assistant Editor **ROXY POLK**
Designer **KAT LARSON**
Digital Production **CHRISTINA McKENZIE**

Special thanks to LEIGH BEACH, GARY CLAY, SHANA DOERR, A.J. RATHBUN, KRISTEN STAR, JEREMY VANHOOZER, and everyone at PopCap Games.

DarkHorse.com | PopCap.com

ABDOPUBLISHING.COM

Reinforced library bound edition published in 2017 by Spotlight, a division of ABDO, PO Box 398166, Minneapolis, Minnesota 55439. Spotlight produces high-quality reinforced library bound editions for schools and libraries.
Published by agreement with Dark Horse Comics.

Printed in the United States of America, North Mankato, Minnesota.
042016
092016

THIS BOOK CONTAINS
RECYCLED MATERIALS

DARK
HORSE
COMICS

PopCap

Originally issued as Plants vs. Zombies #4: Grown Sweet Home Part 1
by Dark Horse Comics in 2015.

PUBLISHER'S CATALOGING IN PUBLICATION DATA

Names: Tobin, Paul, author. | Tong, Andie ; Rainwater, Matthew J., illustrators.
Title: Grown sweet home / by Paul Tobin ; illustrated by Andie Tong and Matthew J. Rainwater.
Description: Minneapolis, MN : Spotlight, [2017] | Series: Plants vs. zombies
Summary: Patrice, Nate, and Crazy Dave give the plants advice on how to act human when they move into Crazy Dave's mansion, but they are unaware that Zomboss is spying on them so he can teach the zombies how to act human.
Identifiers: LCCN 2016934736 | ISBN 9781614795377 (v.1 : lib. bdg.) | ISBN 9781614795384 (v.2 : lib. bdg.) | ISBN 9781614795391 (v.3 : lib. bdg.)
Subjects: LCSH: Plants--Juvenile fiction. | Zombies--Juvenile fiction. | Adventure and adventurers--Juvenile fiction. | Comic books, strips, etc.--Juvenile fiction. | Graphic novels--Juvenile fiction.
Classification: DDC 741.5--dc23
LC record available at http://lccn.loc.gov/2016934736

ABDO
Spotlight

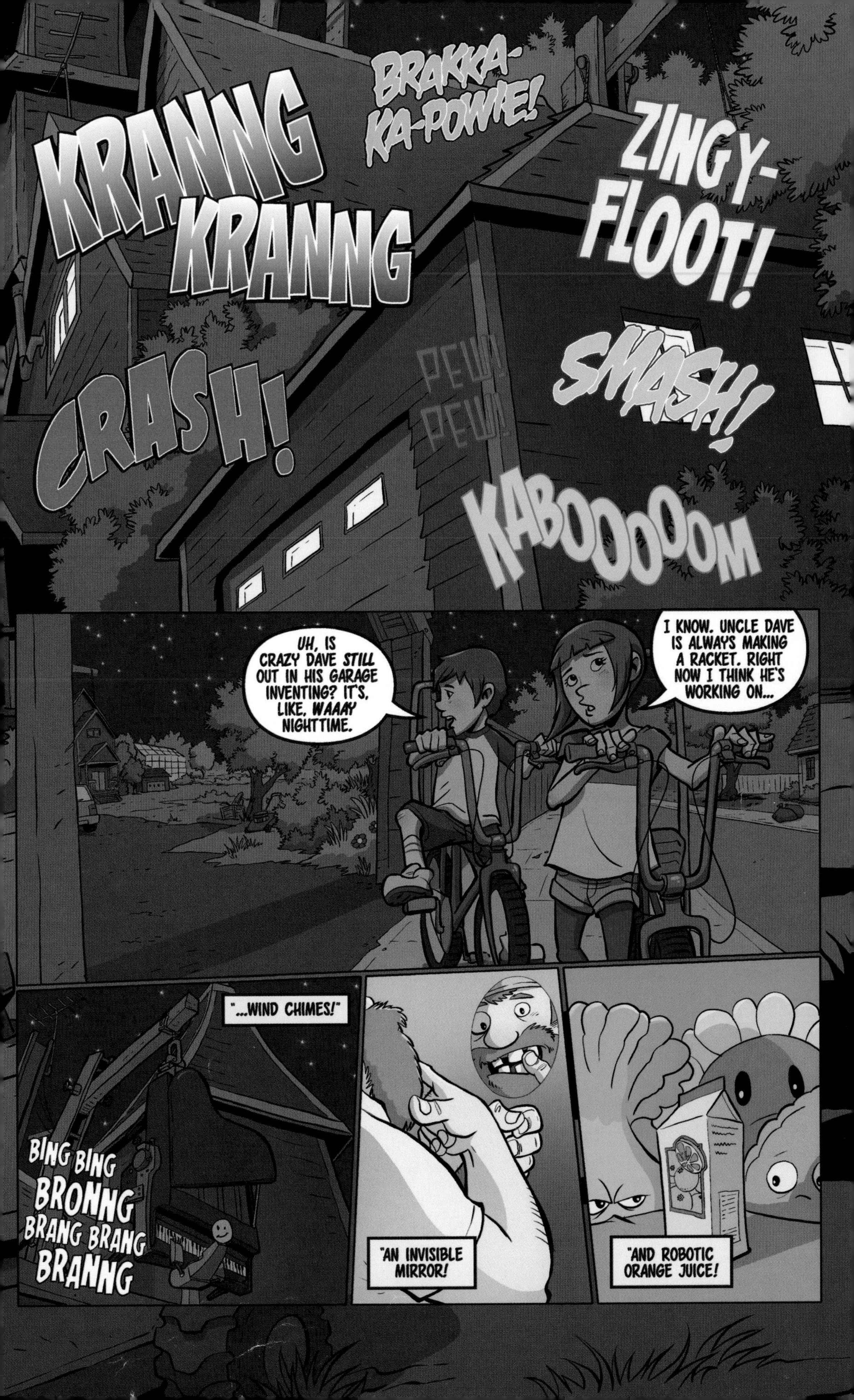

BRAKKA-KA-POWIE!
KRANNG KRANNG
ZINGY-FLOOT!
CRASH!
PEW! PEW!
SMASH!
KABOOOOOM
UH, IS CRAZY DAVE STILL OUT IN HIS GARAGE INVENTING? IT'S, LIKE, WAAAY NIGHTTIME.
I KNOW. UNCLE DAVE IS ALWAYS MAKING A RACKET. RIGHT NOW I THINK HE'S WORKING ON...
"...WIND CHIMES!"
BING BING BRONNG BRANG BRANG BRANNG
"AN INVISIBLE MIRROR!
"AND ROBOTIC ORANGE JUICE!

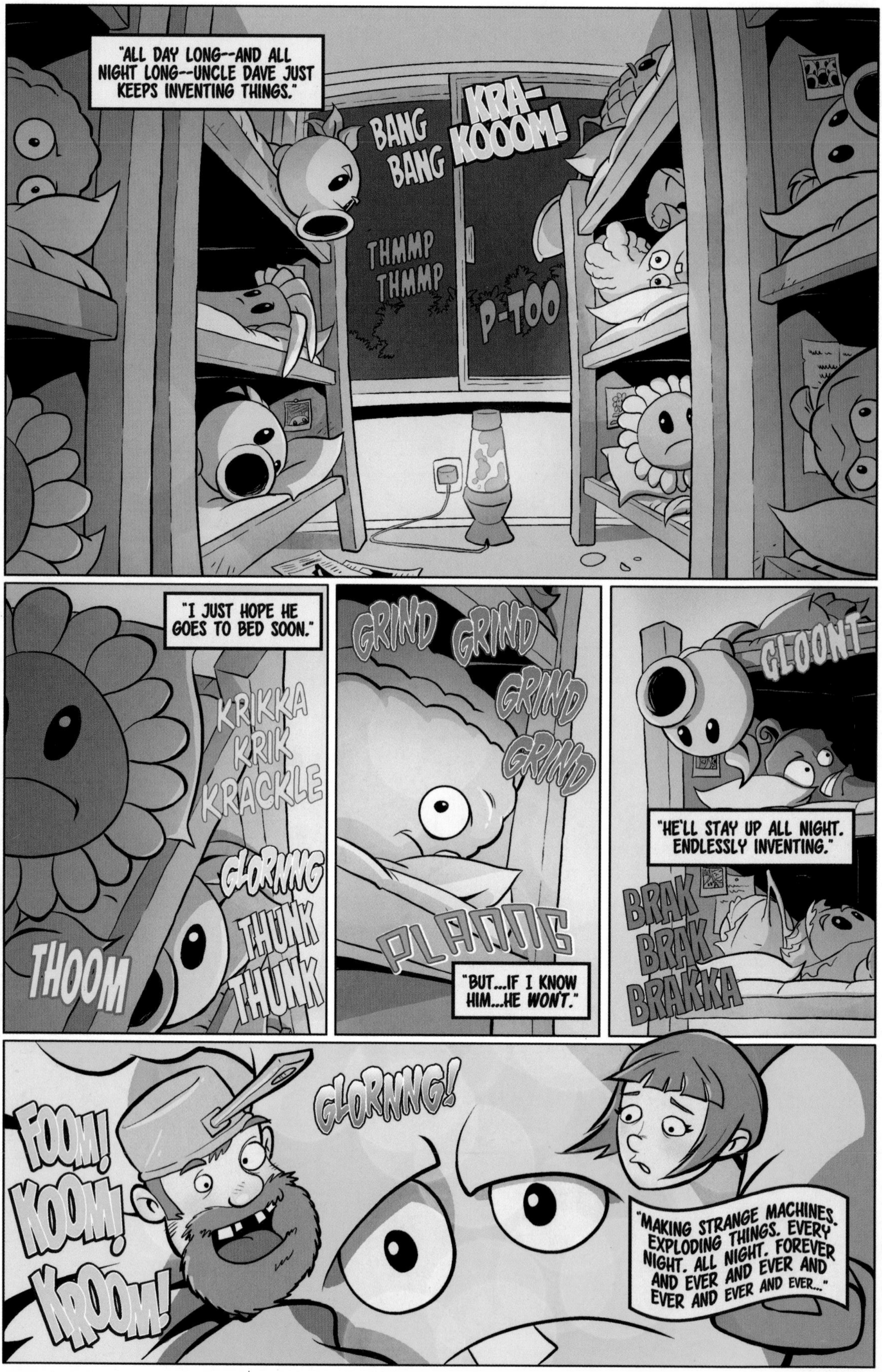
"ALL DAY LONG--AND ALL NIGHT LONG--UNCLE DAVE JUST KEEPS INVENTING THINGS."
BANG BANG
KRA-KOOOM!
THMMP THMMP
P-TOO
"I JUST HOPE HE GOES TO BED SOON."
KRIKKA KRIK KRACKLE
GLORNNG
THUNK THUNK
THOOM
GRIND GRIND GRIND GRIND
PLANNG
"BUT...IF I KNOW HIM...HE *WON'T*."
GLOONT
"HE'LL STAY UP ALL NIGHT. ENDLESSLY INVENTING."
BRAK BRAK BRAKKA
GLORNNG!
FOOM! KOOM! KROOM!
"MAKING STRANGE MACHINES. EXPLODING THINGS. EVERY NIGHT. ALL NIGHT. FOREVER AND EVER AND EVER AND EVER AND EVER AND EVER..."

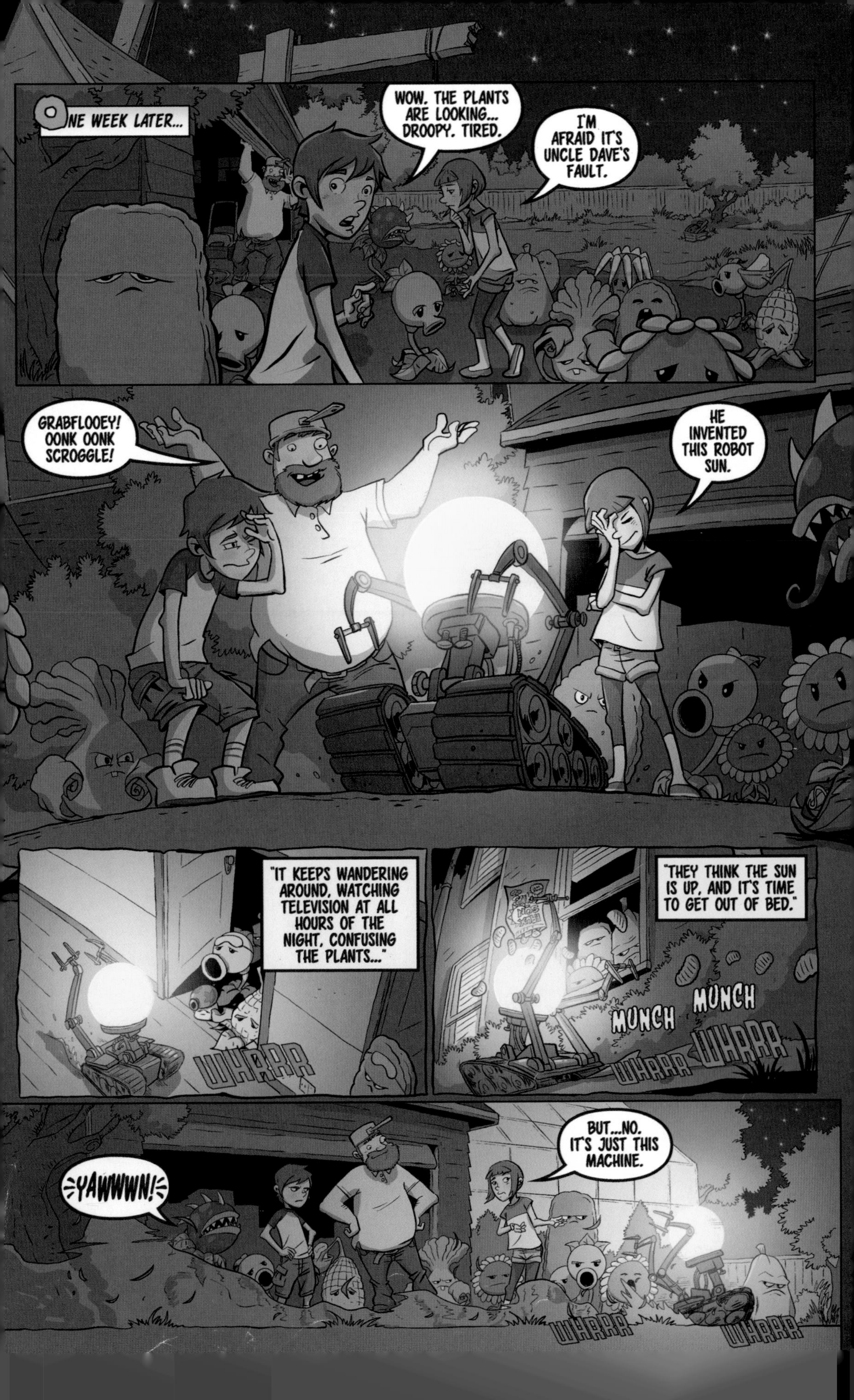
ONE WEEK LATER...
WOW. THE PLANTS ARE LOOKING... DROOPY. TIRED.
I'M AFRAID IT'S UNCLE DAVE'S FAULT.
GRABFLOOEY! OONK OONK SCROGGLE!
HE INVENTED THIS ROBOT SUN.
"IT KEEPS WANDERING AROUND, WATCHING TELEVISION AT ALL HOURS OF THE NIGHT, CONFUSING THE PLANTS..."
WHRRR
"THEY THINK THE SUN IS UP, AND IT'S TIME TO GET OUT OF BED."
MUNCH
MUNCH
WHRRR
WHRRR
YAWWWN!
BUT...NO. IT'S JUST THIS MACHINE.
WHRRR
WHRRR

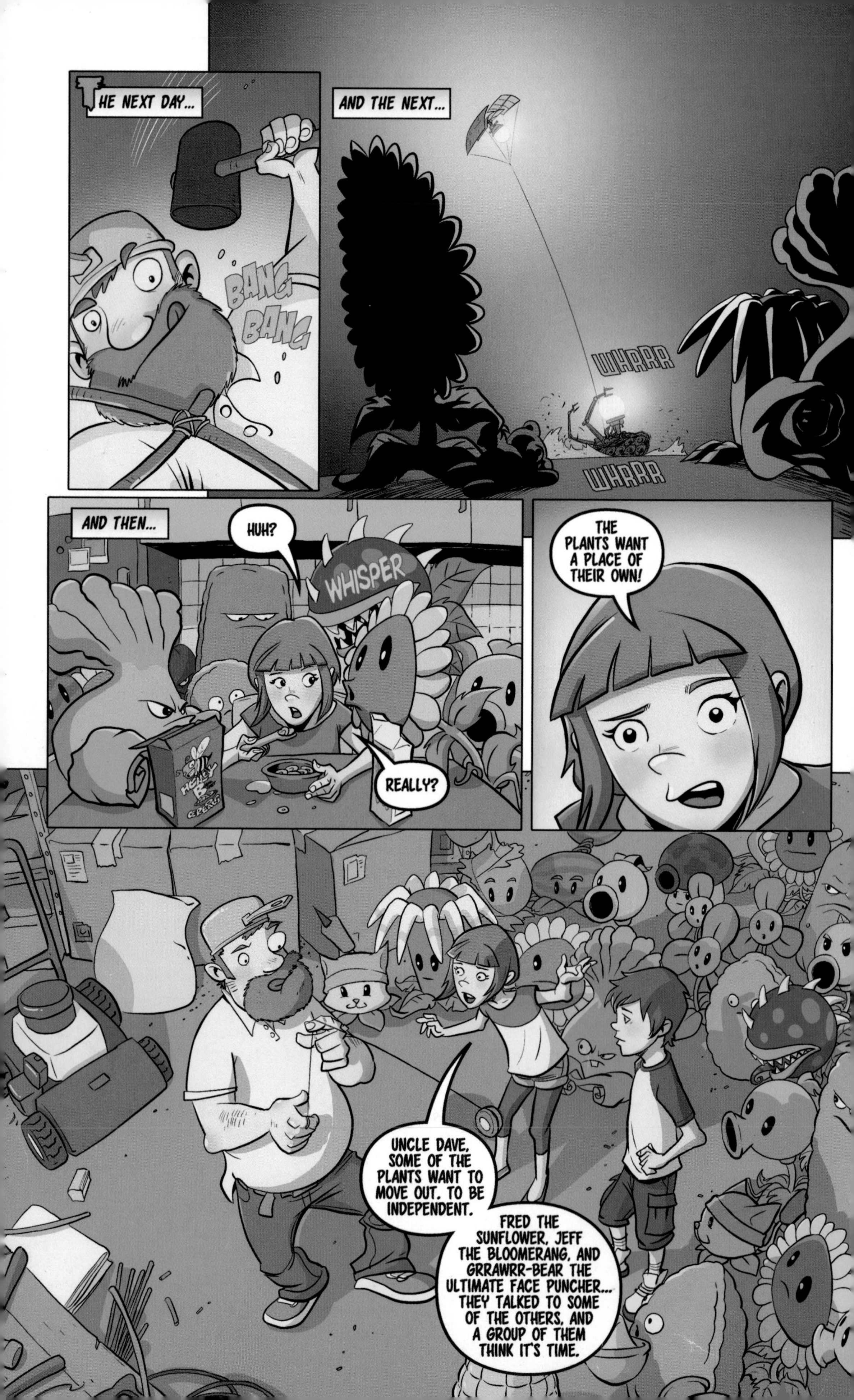
THE NEXT DAY...
BANG
BANG
AND THE NEXT...
WHRRR
WHRRR
AND THEN...
HUH?
WHISPER
HONEY B CEREAL
REALLY?
THE PLANTS WANT A PLACE OF THEIR OWN!
UNCLE DAVE, SOME OF THE PLANTS WANT TO MOVE OUT. TO BE INDEPENDENT.
FRED THE SUNFLOWER, JEFF THE BLOOMERANG, AND GRRAWRR-BEAR THE ULTIMATE FACE PUNCHER... THEY TALKED TO SOME OF THE OTHERS, AND A GROUP OF THEM THINK IT'S TIME.

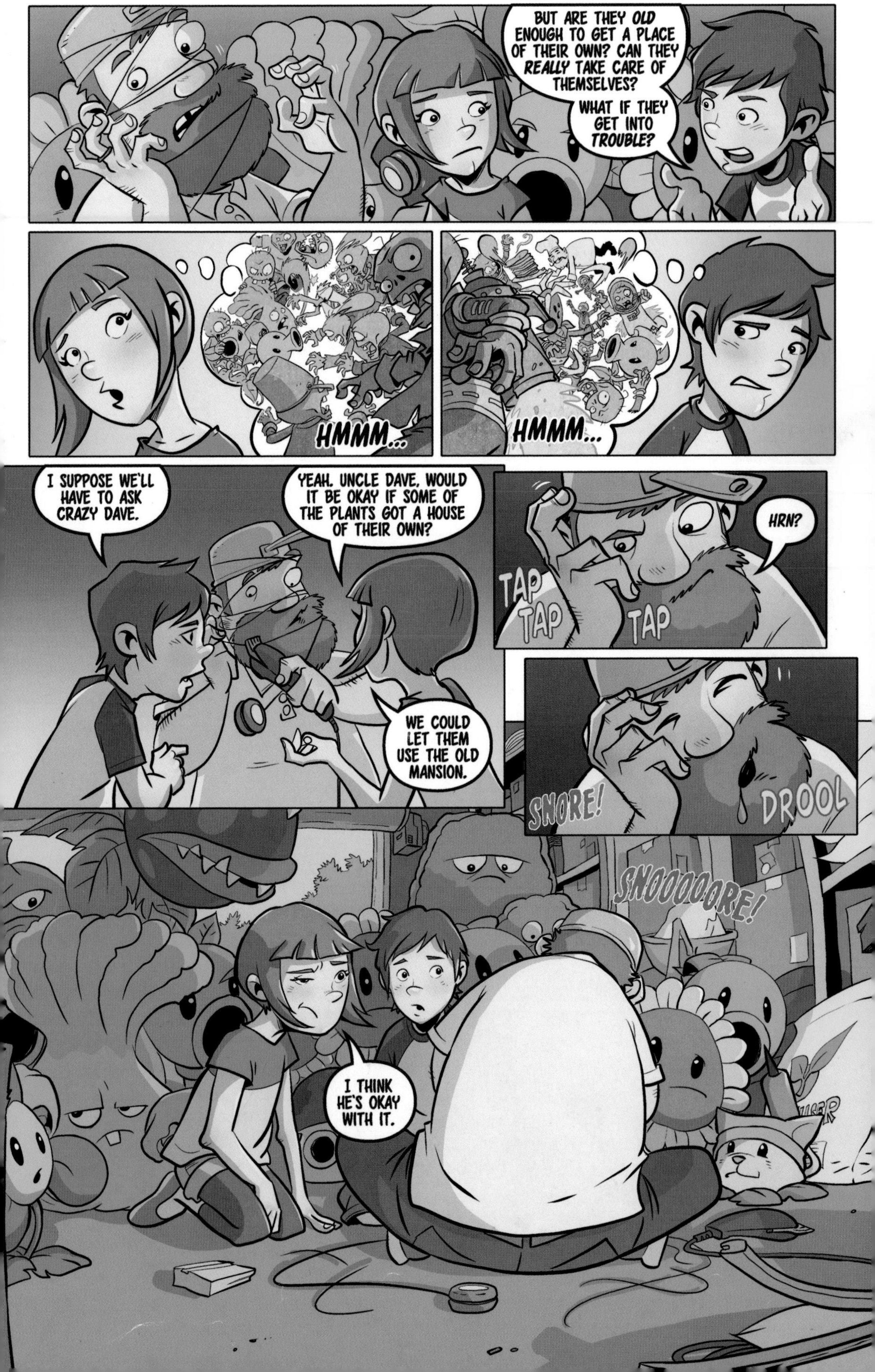

BUT ARE THEY OLD ENOUGH TO GET A PLACE OF THEIR OWN? CAN THEY REALLY TAKE CARE OF THEMSELVES?
WHAT IF THEY GET INTO TROUBLE?
HMMM...
HMMM...
I SUPPOSE WE'LL HAVE TO ASK CRAZY DAVE.
YEAH. UNCLE DAVE, WOULD IT BE OKAY IF SOME OF THE PLANTS GOT A HOUSE OF THEIR OWN?
WE COULD LET THEM USE THE OLD MANSION.
TAP TAP TAP
HRN?
SNORE!
DROOL
SNOOOOORE!
I THINK HE'S OKAY WITH IT.

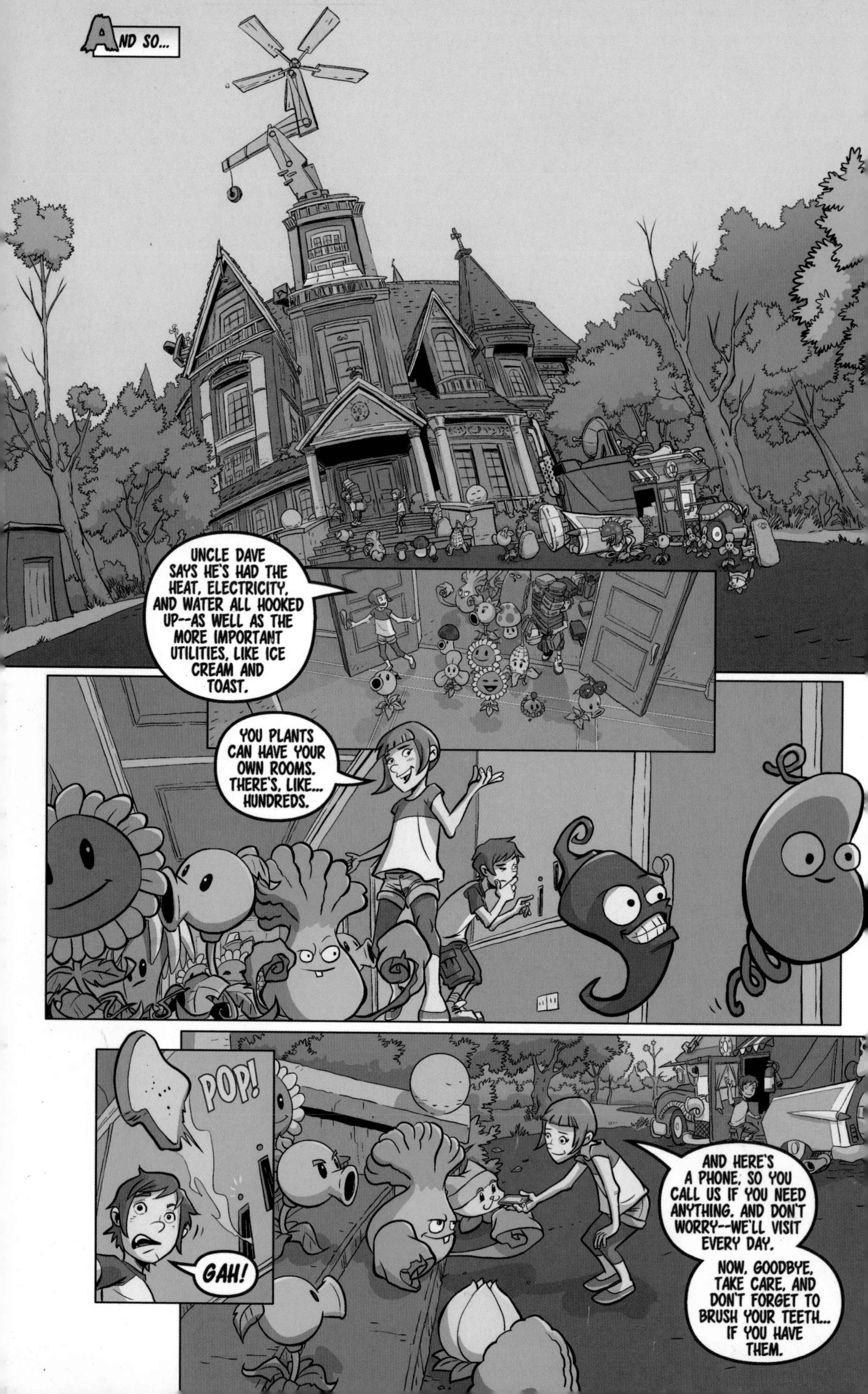
AND SO...
UNCLE DAVE SAYS HE'S HAD THE HEAT, ELECTRICITY, AND WATER ALL HOOKED UP--AS WELL AS THE MORE IMPORTANT UTILITIES, LIKE ICE CREAM AND TOAST.
YOU PLANTS CAN HAVE YOUR OWN ROOMS. THERE'S, LIKE... HUNDREDS.
POP!
GAH!
AND HERE'S A PHONE, SO YOU CALL US IF YOU NEED ANYTHING. AND DON'T WORRY--WE'LL VISIT EVERY DAY.
NOW, GOODBYE, TAKE CARE, AND DON'T FORGET TO BRUSH YOUR TEETH... IF YOU HAVE THEM.

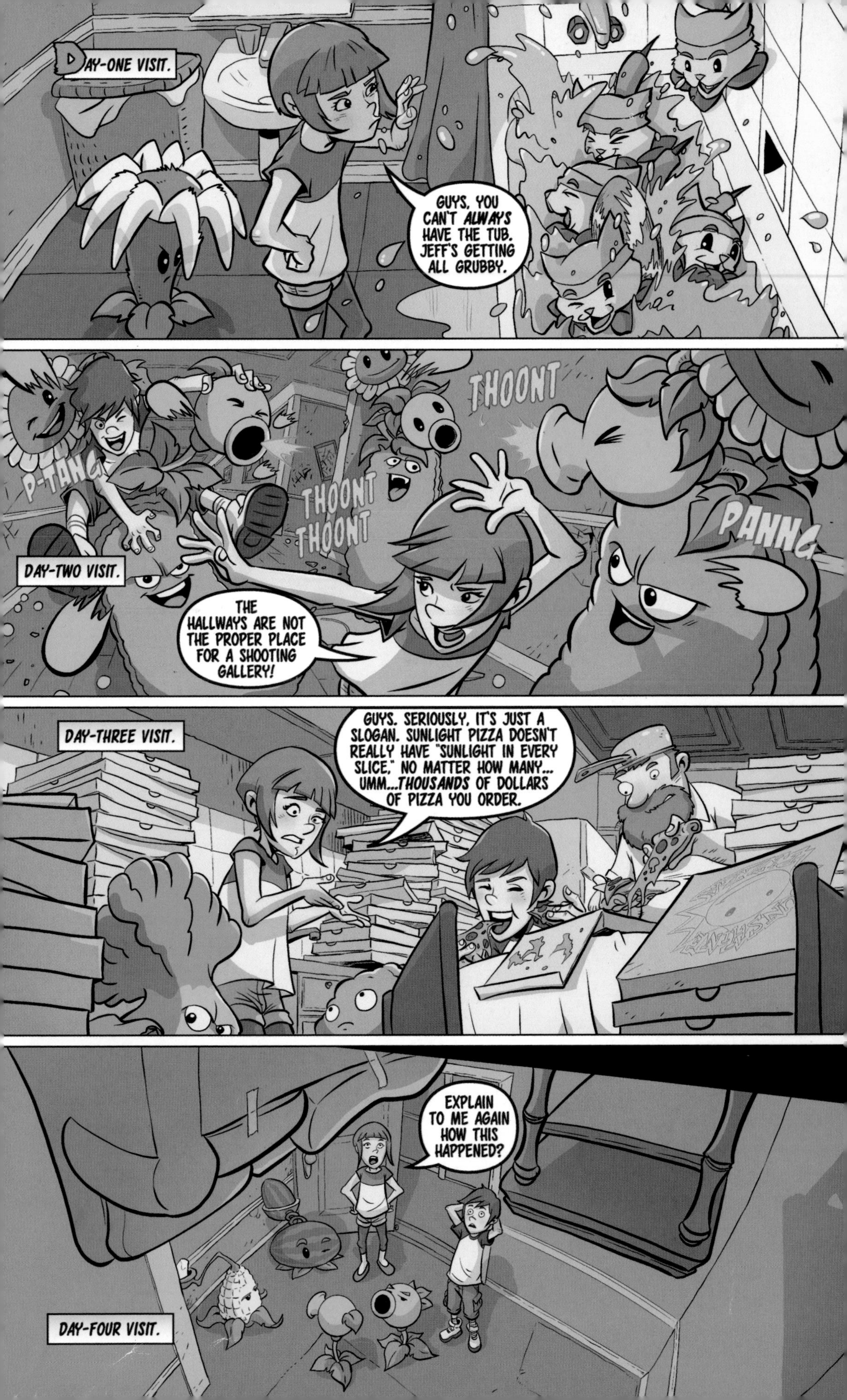
DAY-ONE VISIT.
GUYS, YOU CAN'T *ALWAYS* HAVE THE TUB. JEFF'S GETTING ALL GRUBBY.
DAY-TWO VISIT.
THOONT
P-TANG
THOONT THOONT
PANNG
THE HALLWAYS ARE NOT THE PROPER PLACE FOR A SHOOTING GALLERY!
DAY-THREE VISIT.
GUYS. SERIOUSLY, IT'S JUST A SLOGAN. SUNLIGHT PIZZA DOESN'T REALLY HAVE "SUNLIGHT IN EVERY SLICE," NO MATTER HOW MANY... UMM...*THOUSANDS* OF DOLLARS OF PIZZA YOU ORDER.
DAY-FOUR VISIT.
EXPLAIN TO ME AGAIN HOW THIS HAPPENED?

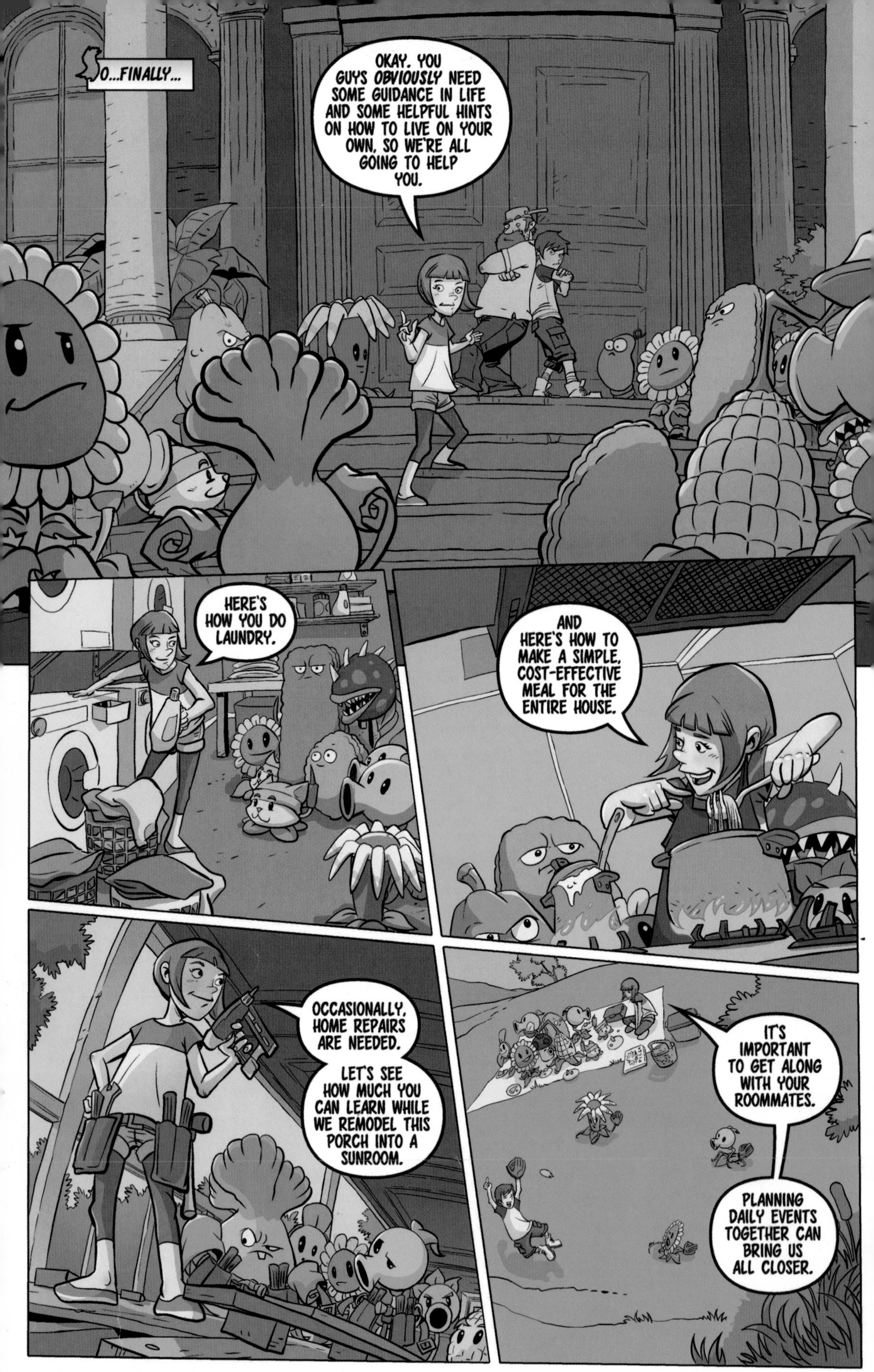
SO...FINALLY...
OKAY. YOU GUYS OBVIOUSLY NEED SOME GUIDANCE IN LIFE AND SOME HELPFUL HINTS ON HOW TO LIVE ON YOUR OWN, SO WE'RE ALL GOING TO HELP YOU.
HERE'S HOW YOU DO LAUNDRY.
AND HERE'S HOW TO MAKE A SIMPLE, COST-EFFECTIVE MEAL FOR THE ENTIRE HOUSE.
OCCASIONALLY, HOME REPAIRS ARE NEEDED.
LET'S SEE HOW MUCH YOU CAN LEARN WHILE WE REMODEL THIS PORCH INTO A SUNROOM.
IT'S IMPORTANT TO GET ALONG WITH YOUR ROOMMATES.
PLANNING DAILY EVENTS TOGETHER CAN BRING US ALL CLOSER.

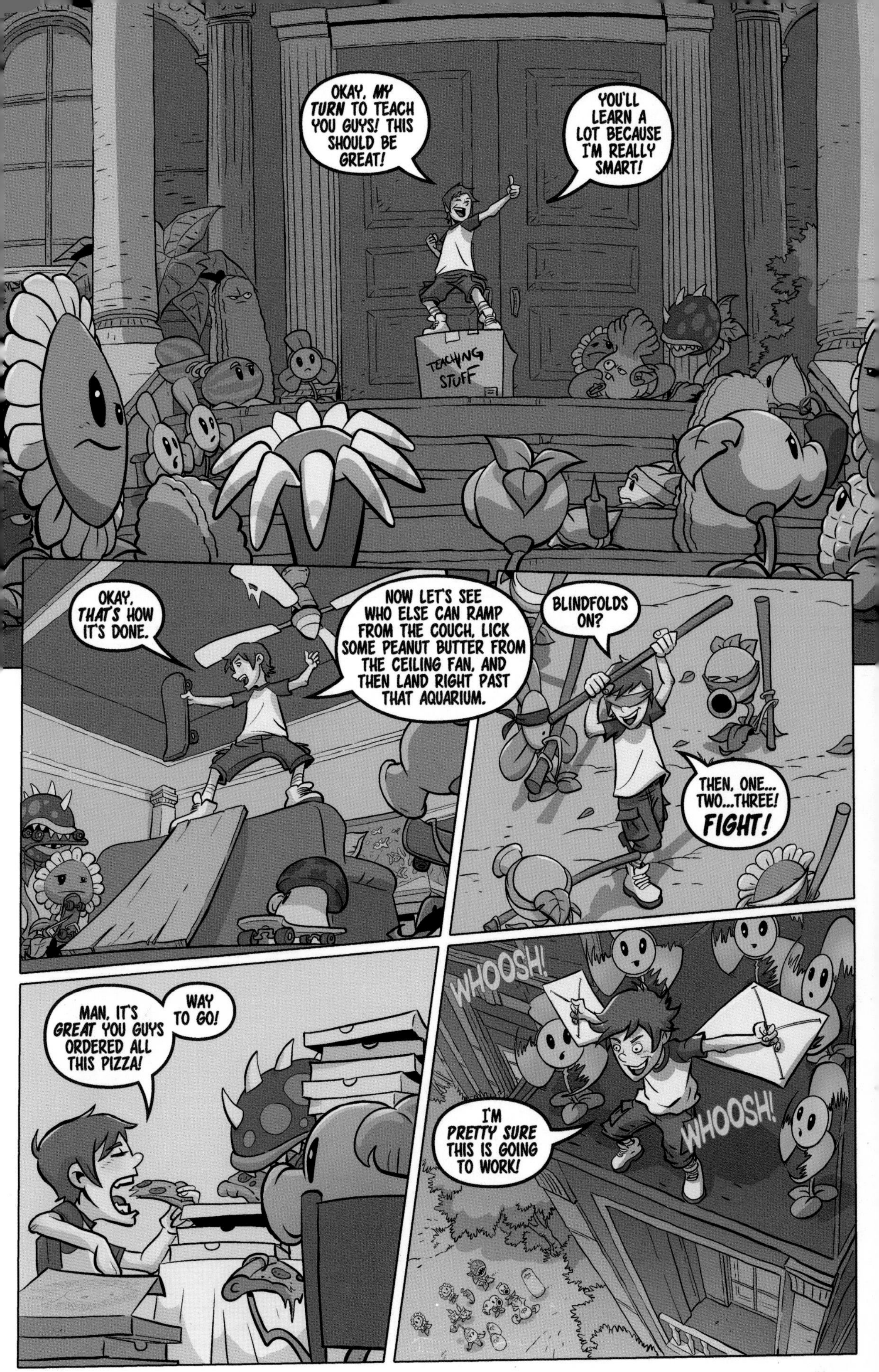
OKAY, MY TURN TO TEACH YOU GUYS! THIS SHOULD BE GREAT!
YOU'LL LEARN A LOT BECAUSE I'M REALLY SMART!
TEACHING STUFF
OKAY, THAT'S HOW IT'S DONE.
NOW LET'S SEE WHO ELSE CAN RAMP FROM THE COUCH, LICK SOME PEANUT BUTTER FROM THE CEILING FAN, AND THEN LAND RIGHT PAST THAT AQUARIUM.
BLINDFOLDS ON?
THEN, ONE... TWO...THREE! FIGHT!
MAN, IT'S GREAT YOU GUYS ORDERED ALL THIS PIZZA!
WAY TO GO!
WHOOSH!
WHOOSH!
I'M PRETTY SURE THIS IS GOING TO WORK!

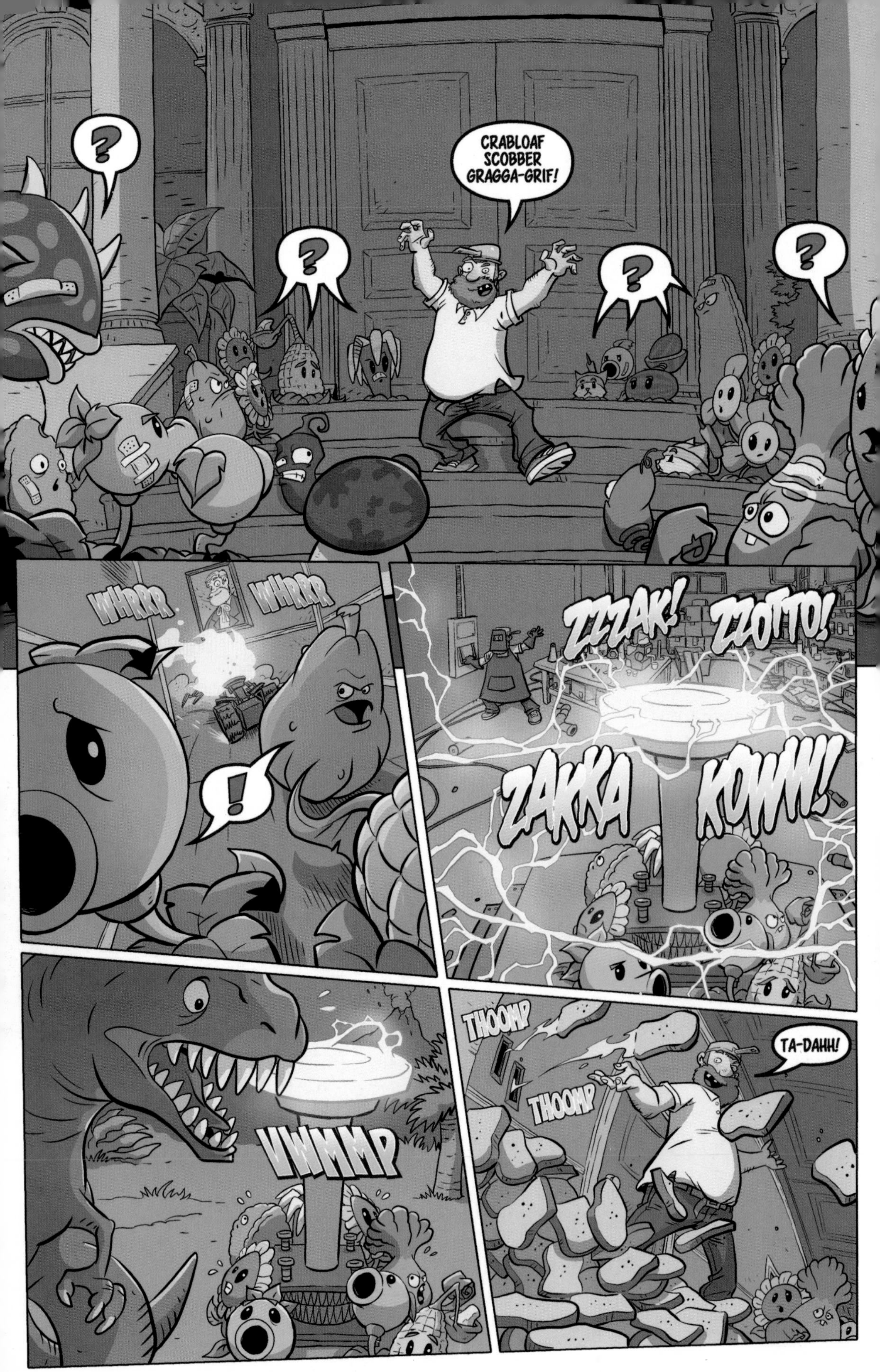
?
CRABLOAF SCOBBER GRAGGA-GRIF!
?
?
?
WHRRR
WHRRR
!
ZZZAK!
ZZOTTO!
ZAKKA
KOWW!
VWMMP
THOOMP
THOOMP
TA-DAHH!

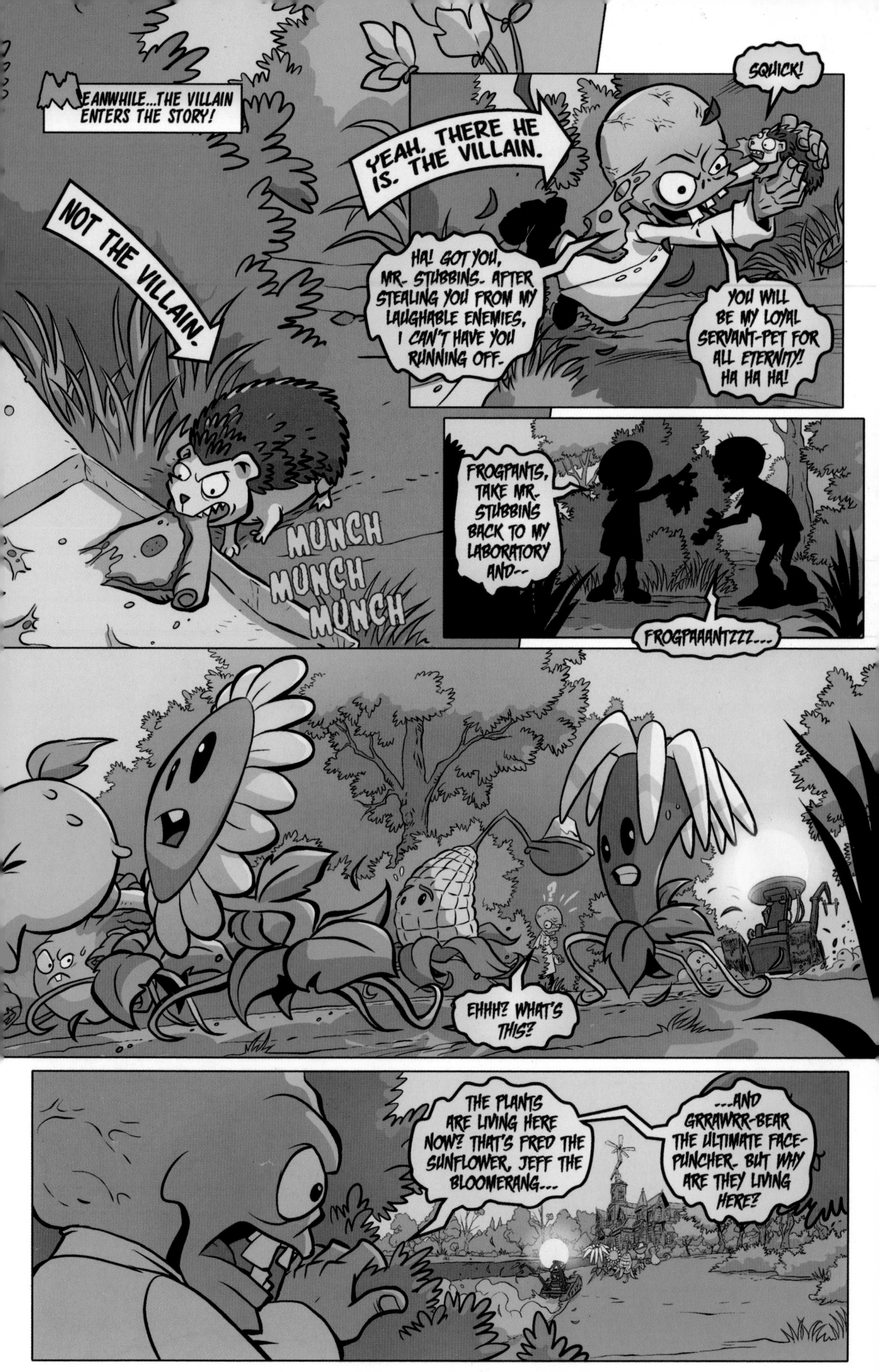
MEANWHILE...THE VILLAIN ENTERS THE STORY!
NOT THE VILLAIN.
YEAH, THERE HE IS. THE VILLAIN.
SQUICK!
HA! GOT YOU, MR. STUBBINS. AFTER STEALING YOU FROM MY LAUGHABLE ENEMIES, I CAN'T HAVE YOU RUNNING OFF.
YOU WILL BE MY LOYAL SERVANT-PET FOR ALL ETERNITY! HA HA HA!
MUNCH MUNCH MUNCH
FROGPANTS, TAKE MR. STUBBINS BACK TO MY LABORATORY AND--
FROGPAAANTZZZ...
EHHH? WHAT'S THIS?
THE PLANTS ARE LIVING HERE NOW? THAT'S FRED THE SUNFLOWER, JEFF THE BLOOMERANG...
...AND GRRAWRR-BEAR THE ULTIMATE FACE-PUNCHER. BUT WHY ARE THEY LIVING HERE?

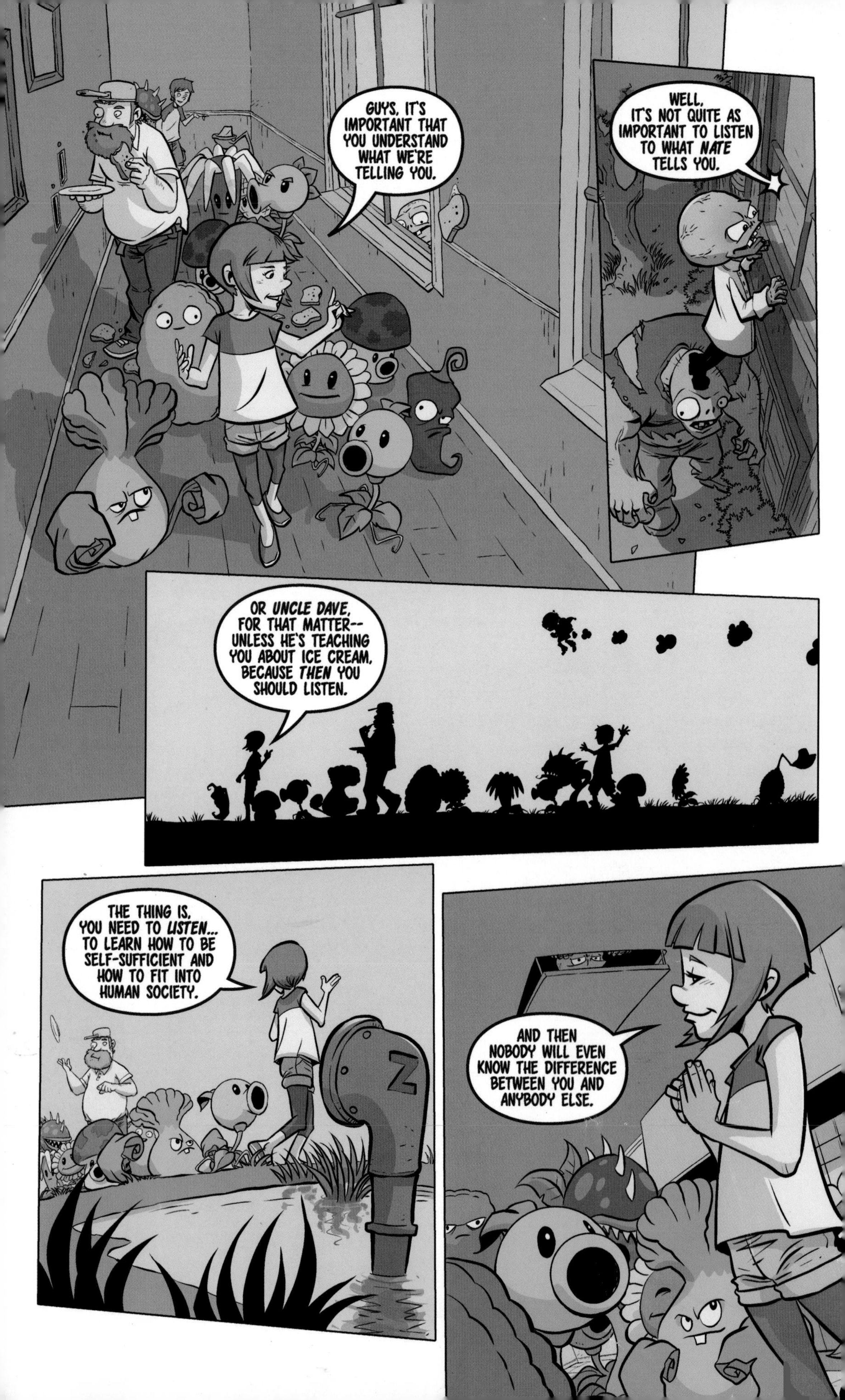
GUYS, IT'S IMPORTANT THAT YOU UNDERSTAND WHAT WE'RE TELLING YOU.
WELL, IT'S NOT QUITE AS IMPORTANT TO LISTEN TO WHAT *NATE* TELLS YOU.
OR *UNCLE DAVE*, FOR THAT MATTER-- UNLESS HE'S TEACHING YOU ABOUT ICE CREAM, BECAUSE *THEN* YOU SHOULD LISTEN.
THE THING IS, YOU NEED TO *LISTEN*... TO LEARN HOW TO BE SELF-SUFFICIENT AND HOW TO FIT INTO HUMAN SOCIETY.
Z
AND THEN NOBODY WILL EVEN KNOW THE DIFFERENCE BETWEEN YOU AND ANYBODY ELSE.

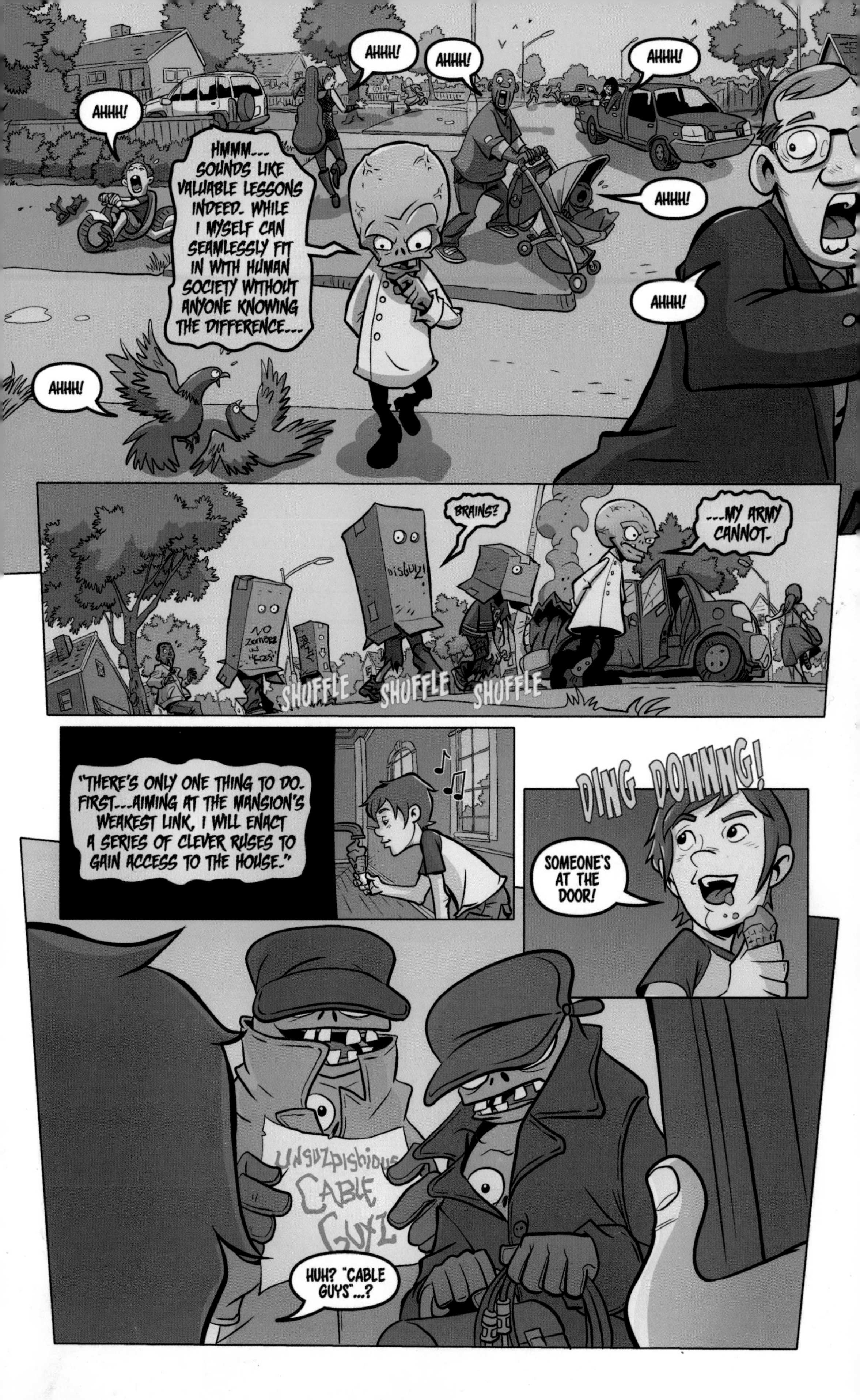

AHHH!
AHHH!
AHHH!
HMMM... SOUNDS LIKE VALUABLE LESSONS INDEED. WHILE I MYSELF CAN SEAMLESSLY FIT IN WITH HUMAN SOCIETY WITHOUT ANYONE KNOWING THE DIFFERENCE...
AHHH!
AHHH!
AHHH!
AHHH!
BRAINS?
...MY ARMY CANNOT.
SHUFFLE
SHUFFLE
SHUFFLE
"THERE'S ONLY ONE THING TO DO. FIRST...AIMING AT THE MANSION'S WEAKEST LINK, I WILL ENACT A SERIES OF CLEVER RUSES TO GAIN ACCESS TO THE HOUSE."
DING DONNNG!
SOMEONE'S AT THE DOOR!
UNSUZPISHIOUS CABLE GUYZ
HUH? "CABLE GUYS"...?

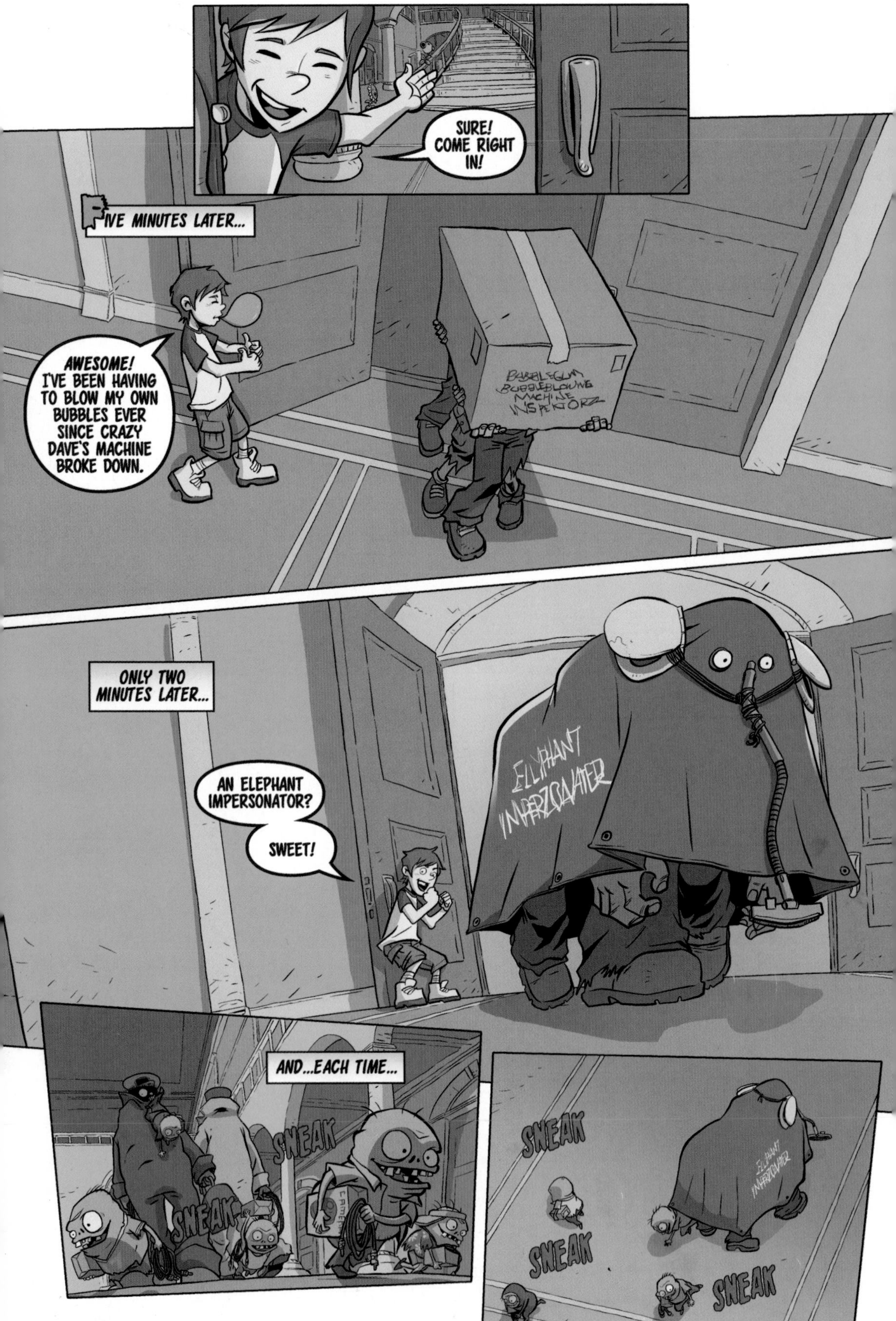
SURE! COME RIGHT IN!
FIVE MINUTES LATER...
AWESOME! I'VE BEEN HAVING TO BLOW MY OWN BUBBLES EVER SINCE CRAZY DAVE'S MACHINE BROKE DOWN.
BUBBLEGUM BUBBLEBLOWING MACHINE INSPEKTORZ
ONLY TWO MINUTES LATER...
AN ELEPHANT IMPERSONATOR?
SWEET!
ELLYPHANT INPERZONATER
AND...EACH TIME...
SNEAK
SNEAK
SNEAK
SNEAK
SNEAK

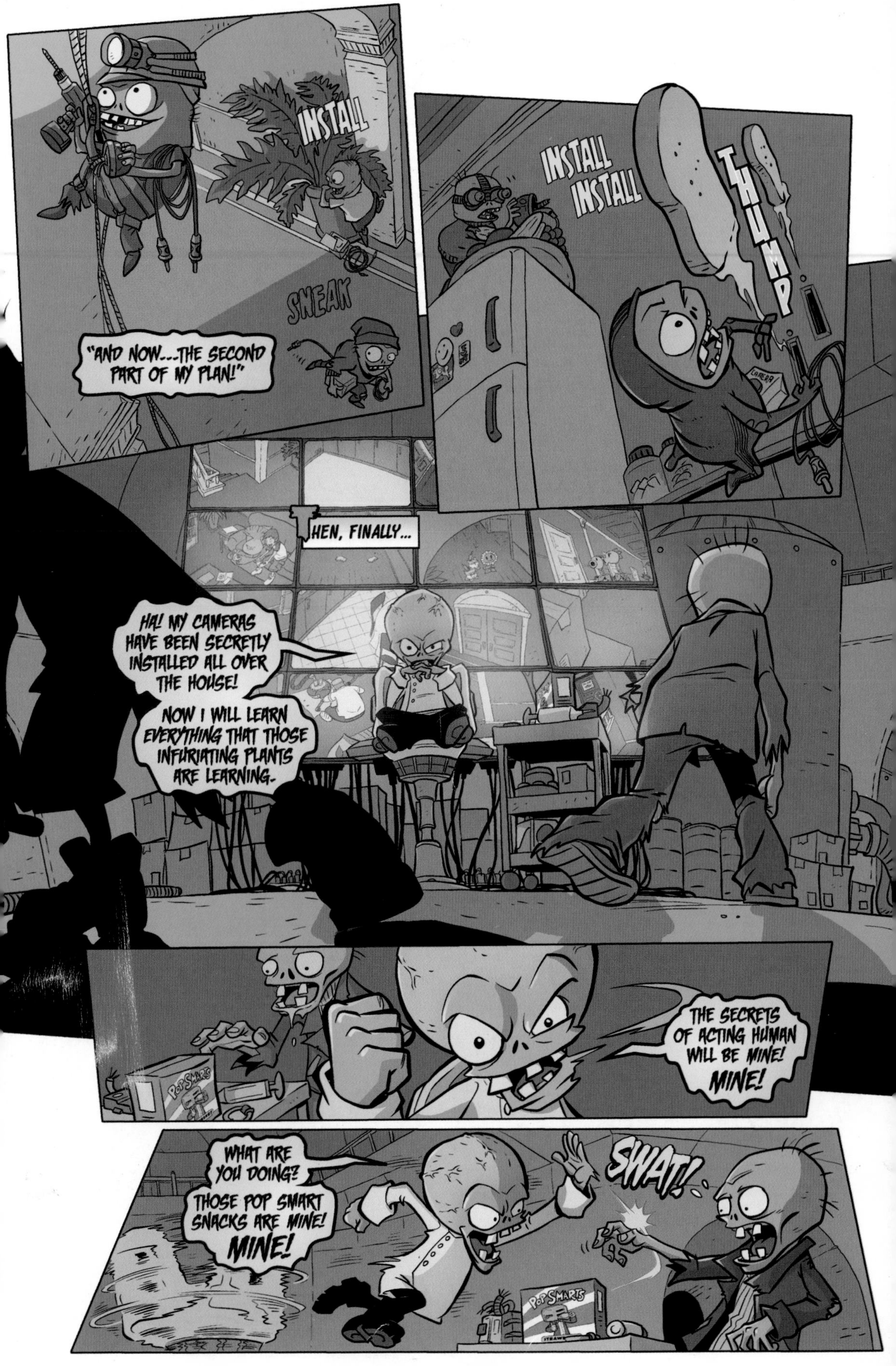
INSTALL
SNEAK
"AND NOW...THE SECOND PART OF MY PLAN!"
INSTALL INSTALL
THUMP
THEN, FINALLY...
HA! MY CAMERAS HAVE BEEN SECRETLY INSTALLED ALL OVER THE HOUSE!
NOW I WILL LEARN EVERYTHING THAT THOSE INFURIATING PLANTS ARE LEARNING.
THE SECRETS OF ACTING HUMAN WILL BE MINE! MINE!
WHAT ARE YOU DOING?
THOSE POP SMART SNACKS ARE MINE! MINE!
SWAT!

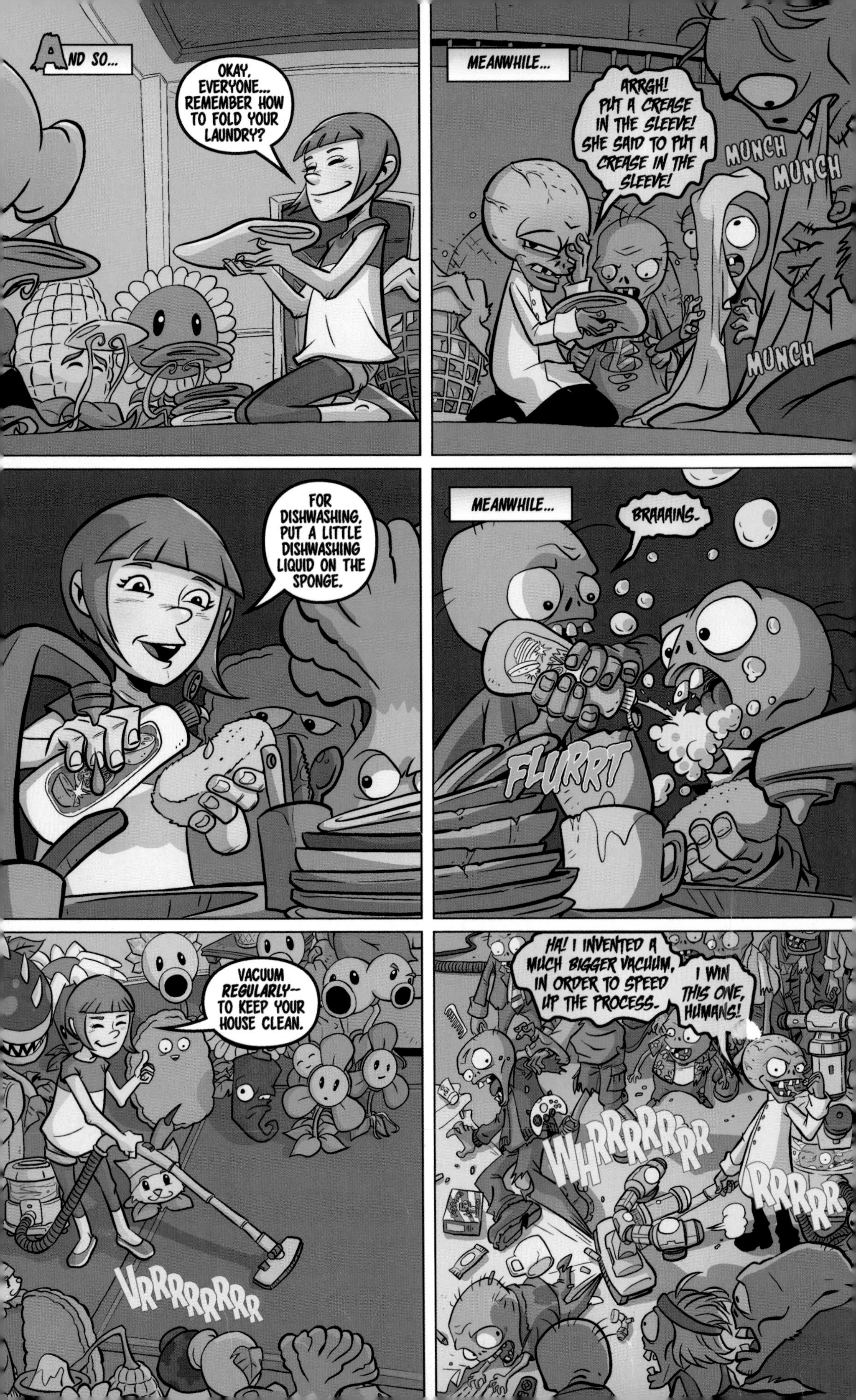
AND SO...
OKAY, EVERYONE... REMEMBER HOW TO FOLD YOUR LAUNDRY?
MEANWHILE...
ARRGH! PUT A CREASE IN THE SLEEVE! SHE SAID TO PUT A CREASE IN THE SLEEVE!
MUNCH
MUNCH
MUNCH
FOR DISHWASHING, PUT A LITTLE DISHWASHING LIQUID ON THE SPONGE.
MEANWHILE...
BRAAAINS.
FLURRT
VACUUM REGULARLY--TO KEEP YOUR HOUSE CLEAN.
VRRRRRRRRR
HA! I INVENTED A MUCH BIGGER VACUUM, IN ORDER TO SPEED UP THE PROCESS.
I WIN THIS ONE, HUMANS!
WHRRRRRRRR
RRRRR

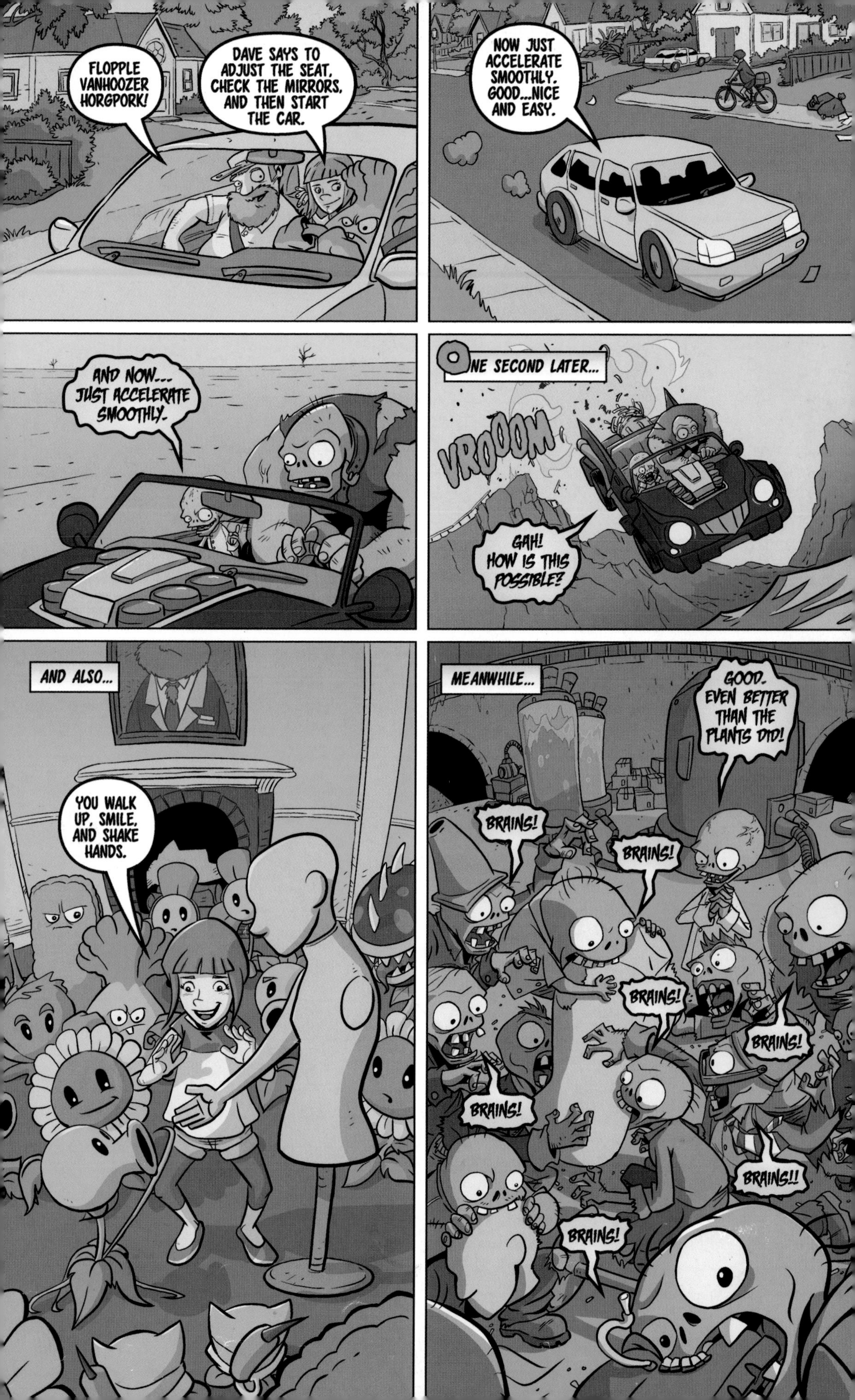
FLOPPLE VANHOOZER HORGPORK!
DAVE SAYS TO ADJUST THE SEAT, CHECK THE MIRRORS, AND THEN START THE CAR.
NOW JUST ACCELERATE SMOOTHLY. GOOD...NICE AND EASY.
AND NOW... JUST ACCELERATE SMOOTHLY.
ONE SECOND LATER...
VROOOM
GAH! HOW IS THIS POSSIBLE?
AND ALSO...
YOU WALK UP, SMILE, AND SHAKE HANDS.
MEANWHILE...
GOOD. EVEN BETTER THAN THE PLANTS DID!
BRAINS!
BRAINS!
BRAINS!
BRAINS!
BRAINS!
BRAINS!!
BRAINS!

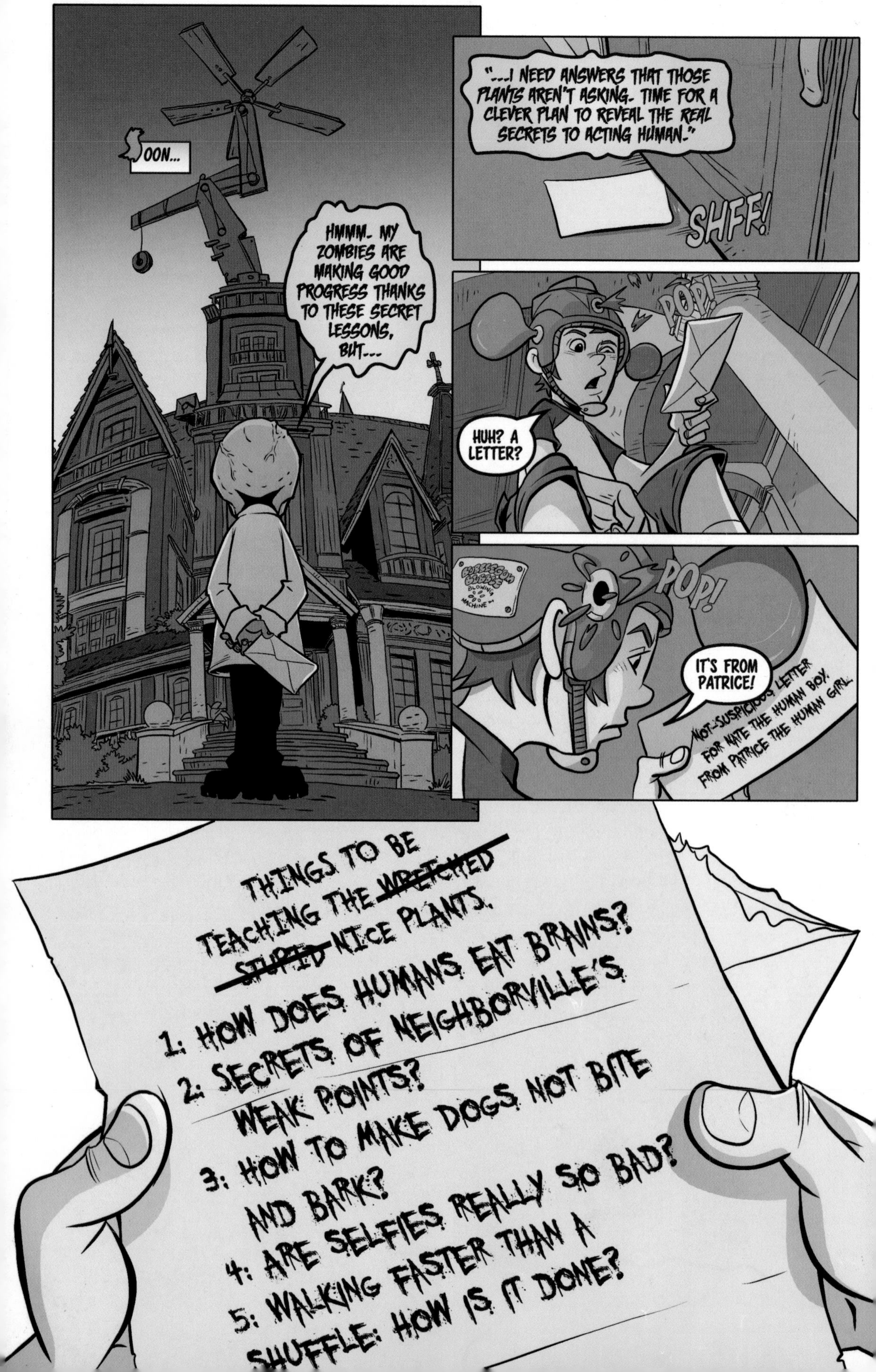
SOON...
HMMM. MY ZOMBIES ARE MAKING GOOD PROGRESS THANKS TO THESE SECRET LESSONS, BUT...
"...I NEED ANSWERS THAT THOSE PLANTS AREN'T ASKING. TIME FOR A CLEVER PLAN TO REVEAL THE REAL SECRETS TO ACTING HUMAN."
SHFF!
POP!
HUH? A LETTER?
BLOWING MACHINE
POP!
IT'S FROM PATRICE!
NOT-SUSPICIOUS LETTER FOR NATE THE HUMAN BOY. FROM PATRICE THE HUMAN GIRL.
THINGS TO BE TEACHING THE ~~WRETCHED~~ ~~STUPID~~ NICE PLANTS.
1: HOW DOES HUMANS EAT BRAINS?
2: SECRETS OF NEIGHBORVILLE'S WEAK POINTS?
3: HOW TO MAKE DOGS NOT BITE AND BARK?
4: ARE SELFIES REALLY SO BAD?
5: WALKING FASTER THAN A SHUFFLE: HOW IS IT DONE?

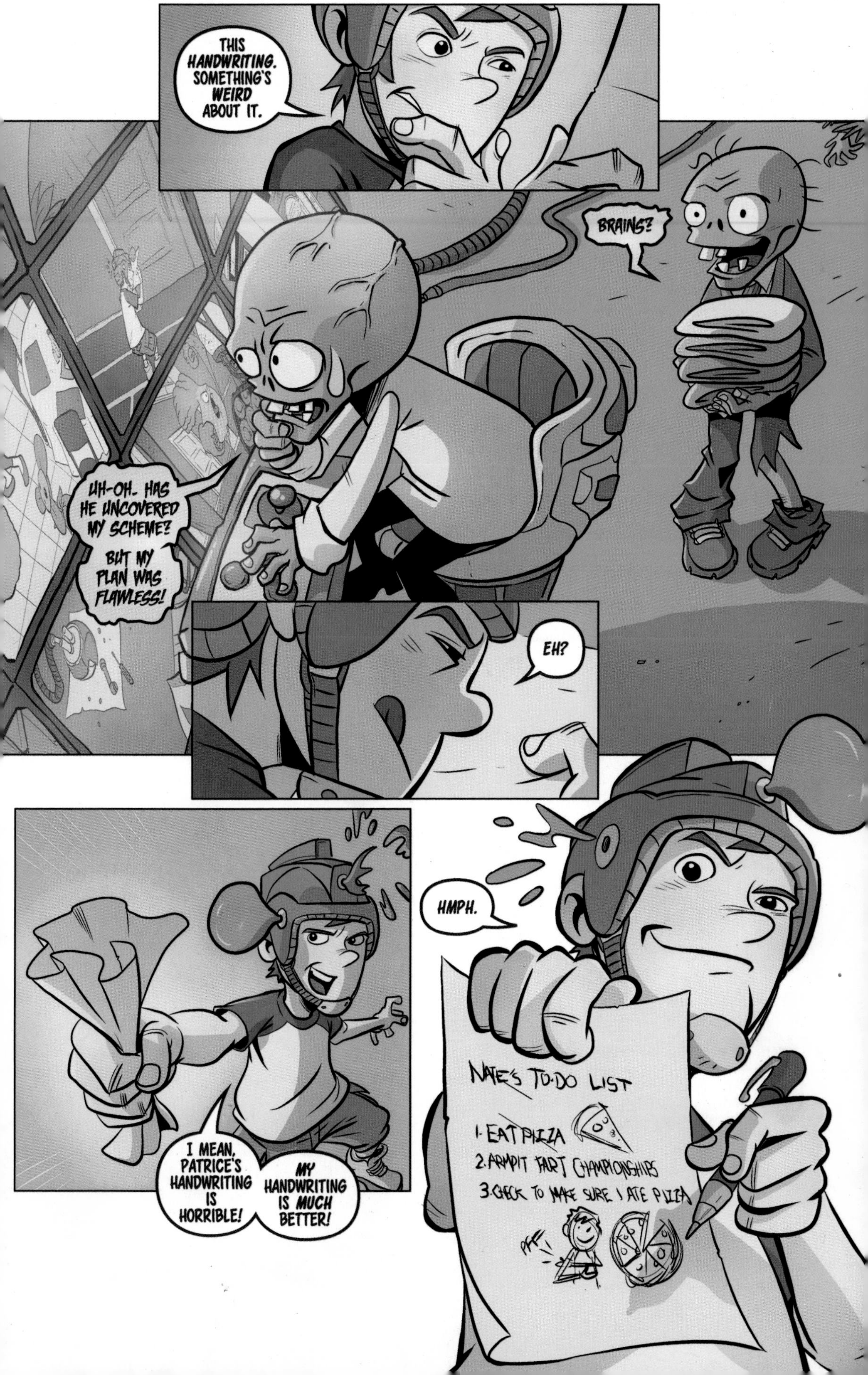
THIS HANDWRITING. SOMETHING'S WEIRD ABOUT IT.
BRAINS?
UH-OH. HAS HE UNCOVERED MY SCHEME?
BUT MY PLAN WAS FLAWLESS!
EH?
I MEAN, PATRICE'S HANDWRITING IS HORRIBLE!
MY HANDWRITING IS MUCH BETTER!
HMPH.
NATE'S TO-DO LIST
1. EAT PIZZA
2. ARMPIT FART CHAMPIONSHIPS
3. CHECK TO MAKE SURE I ATE PIZZA
PFFF!

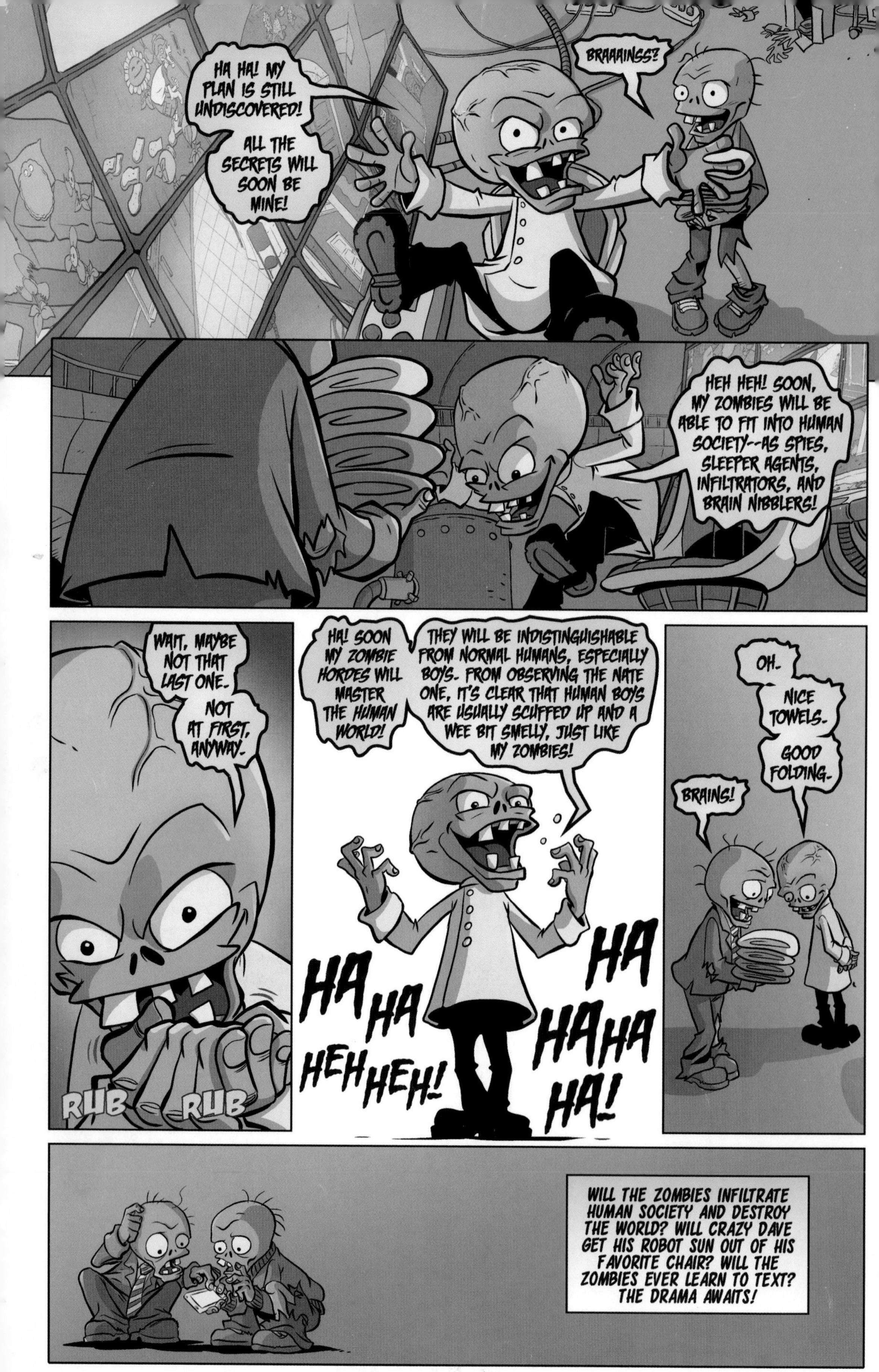
HA HA! MY PLAN IS STILL UNDISCOVERED!
ALL THE SECRETS WILL SOON BE MINE!
BRAAAINSS?
HEH HEH! SOON, MY ZOMBIES WILL BE ABLE TO FIT INTO HUMAN SOCIETY--AS SPIES, SLEEPER AGENTS, INFILTRATORS, AND BRAIN NIBBLERS!
WAIT, MAYBE NOT THAT LAST ONE.
NOT AT FIRST, ANYWAY.
RUB RUB
HA! SOON MY ZOMBIE HORDES WILL MASTER THE HUMAN WORLD!
THEY WILL BE INDISTINGUISHABLE FROM NORMAL HUMANS, ESPECIALLY BOYS. FROM OBSERVING THE NATE ONE, IT'S CLEAR THAT HUMAN BOYS ARE USUALLY SCUFFED UP AND A WEE BIT SMELLY, JUST LIKE MY ZOMBIES!
HA HA HEH HEH!
HA HA HA HA!
OH.
NICE TOWELS.
GOOD FOLDING.
BRAINS!
WILL THE ZOMBIES INFILTRATE HUMAN SOCIETY AND DESTROY THE WORLD? WILL CRAZY DAVE GET HIS ROBOT SUN OUT OF HIS FAVORITE CHAIR? WILL THE ZOMBIES EVER LEARN TO TEXT? THE DRAMA AWAITS!